THIS WALKER BOOK BELONGS TO:

_____

_____

_____

_____

For the real boss,
Sam Hest

A.H.

For Sophie
and the new baby

J.B.

First published 1997 by Walker Books Ltd
87 Vauxhall Walk, London SE11 5HJ

This edition published 1999

2 4 6 8 10 9 7 5 3

Text © 1997 Amy Hest
Illustrations © 1997 Jill Barton

This book has been typeset in
Opti Lucius Ad Bold.

Printed in Hong Kong

British Library Cataloguing in Publication Data
A catalogue record for this book is
available from the British Library.

ISBN 0-7445-6305-4

You're the Boss,
Baby Duck!

written by **Amy Hest**

illustrated by **Jill Barton**

WALKER BOOKS
AND SUBSIDIARIES
LONDON • BOSTON • SYDNEY

Baby Duck was having a bad day.
There was a brand-new baby in the house,
and everyone was making a great big fuss
for no good reason.

"What a fine little face," cooed Mrs Duck.

"Don't you love her little beak?"

"No," Baby said.

"What fine little feet," trilled Mr Duck.

"Isn't she hot stuff?"

"No," Baby said.

Baby Duck sat by herself. She sang a little song.

"Send that no-good Hot Stuff back,
No one wants her here.
Her beak is fat, her feet are fat,
And I'm the only baby."

"Are you singing to your baby sister?"
called Mr Duck. "What a fine sister you are!"
Baby stopped singing.

Baby got up and hopped on
one foot. "Look at me!"

Mrs Duck kissed Hot Stuff on her
fat little beak. She forgot to look.

Baby rolled over.

"Look at me!"

Mr Duck tickled Hot Stuff on her
fat little feet. He forgot to look.

Baby Duck turned
pages in her book.
"I can read,"
she said.

Mrs Duck put Hot Stuff into Baby's old coat.

Mr Duck tucked
Hot Stuff into
Baby's old
pram.

They did not hear her read.

"Time to show Grandpa your brand-new baby sister!" called Mr and Mrs Duck.

Baby Duck stomped along. She dragged her feet and mumbled.

"That bad baby is in my pram,
Wearing my nice coat.
I hope she goes away today
And stays away for ever."

Grandpa was waiting at the kitchen door.

He looked in the pram.

"Welcome," he said.

Then he kissed Baby's cheeks.

"Bad day?" he asked.

"Yes," Baby said.

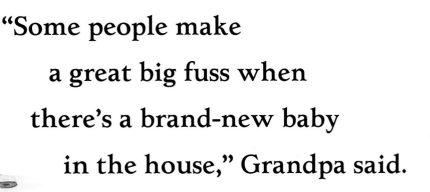

"Some people make
a great big fuss when
there's a brand-new baby
in the house," Grandpa said.

"Yes," Baby said.

"I am making lunch," Grandpa
said. "Want to help?"

"Yes," Baby said.

Baby Duck and Grandpa made lemonade.

Grandpa squeezed lemons.

Baby poured sugar.

"You are a good helper," Grandpa said.

"Brand-new babies are bad helpers,"
Baby said.

"Oh, yes," Grandpa said. "Brand-new babies
don't do much. They don't know how."

Baby Duck and Grandpa made sandwiches
with jam. Baby fetched the bread. Grandpa
chose some jam.

"Not that jam," Baby said. "*That* one."

"You're the boss, Baby Duck," Grandpa said.

"Yes," Baby said. "I am!"

The sandwiches were a big hit.

And, of course, the lemonade.

After lunch Baby put Hot Stuff
in her trolley.

"No crying," Baby said. "I'm the boss."

Hot Stuff did not cry.

"Look at me!"

Baby hopped on one foot.

Hot Stuff looked.

She gurgled.

"Look at me!" Baby rolled over.

Hot Stuff looked.

She burbled.

"Now I will read you a story."
Baby turned pages
in her book.

Hot Stuff gurgled. She giggled and
burbled and babbled.

After that, Baby Duck pulled Hot Stuff all round the garden. She sang a little song:

"Brand-new babies are a pain:
Fuss, fuss, fuss, fuss, fuss.
Maybe you can stay two days
But Baby Duck is boss!"

MORE WALKER PAPERBACKS
For You to Enjoy

Also by Amy Hest

IN THE RAIN WITH BABY DUCK
illustrated by Jill Barton

Baby Duck hates the rain. Mother and Father Duck can't
understand it. But Grandpa can and he knows
how to make Baby happy!

"Brilliant combination of text and pictures…
A night after night book for two to four-year-olds." *The Sunday Telegraph*

0-7445-5234-6   £5.99

ROSIE'S FISHING TRIP
illustrated by Paul Howard

"The harmony between the old and the very young has not often
been shown as effectively as it is here…
Little girls will love this one." *The Junior Bookshelf*

0-7445-4703-2   £4.99

JAMAICA LOUISE JAMES
illustrated by Sheila White Samton

Jamaica Louise James lives in New York with her Mama and Grammy
and she loves to draw and tell stories about the things she sees around her.
This colourful story tells of her big, cool idea for brightening up Grammy's birthday.

0-7445-5293-1   £4.99